ABANDON ✝ SHIP

All photos shot one week in New York City, by Dave Schubert.

These days too many people are taking pictures and too and too many pictures are being taken due to the cell phone cameras, digital cameras, and the surveillance that is being done today. This is an evil technological age that we are living in. I also feel that the majority of the people taking these pictures are driven by impure motives. However, I am very pleased to inform you that Dave Schubert exists, and is taking pictures, and has been for quite some time. Dave is a rare being. I don't think of him as a photographer, because to me that's a lame professional word used by corporations. He uses his eyes, his heart, and his hands to make epic pictures. Dave Schubert is a see-er.

Dash Snow

Abandon Ship By Dave Schubert

Published by Seems

1777 Yosemite Ave. Suite 360
San Francisco California 94124 USA
Copyright 2005 Seems Right
seemsrightcollections.com

First edition, published December 2005

Printed in the USA

ISBN 1-59975-368-5

ABANDON
†
SHIP

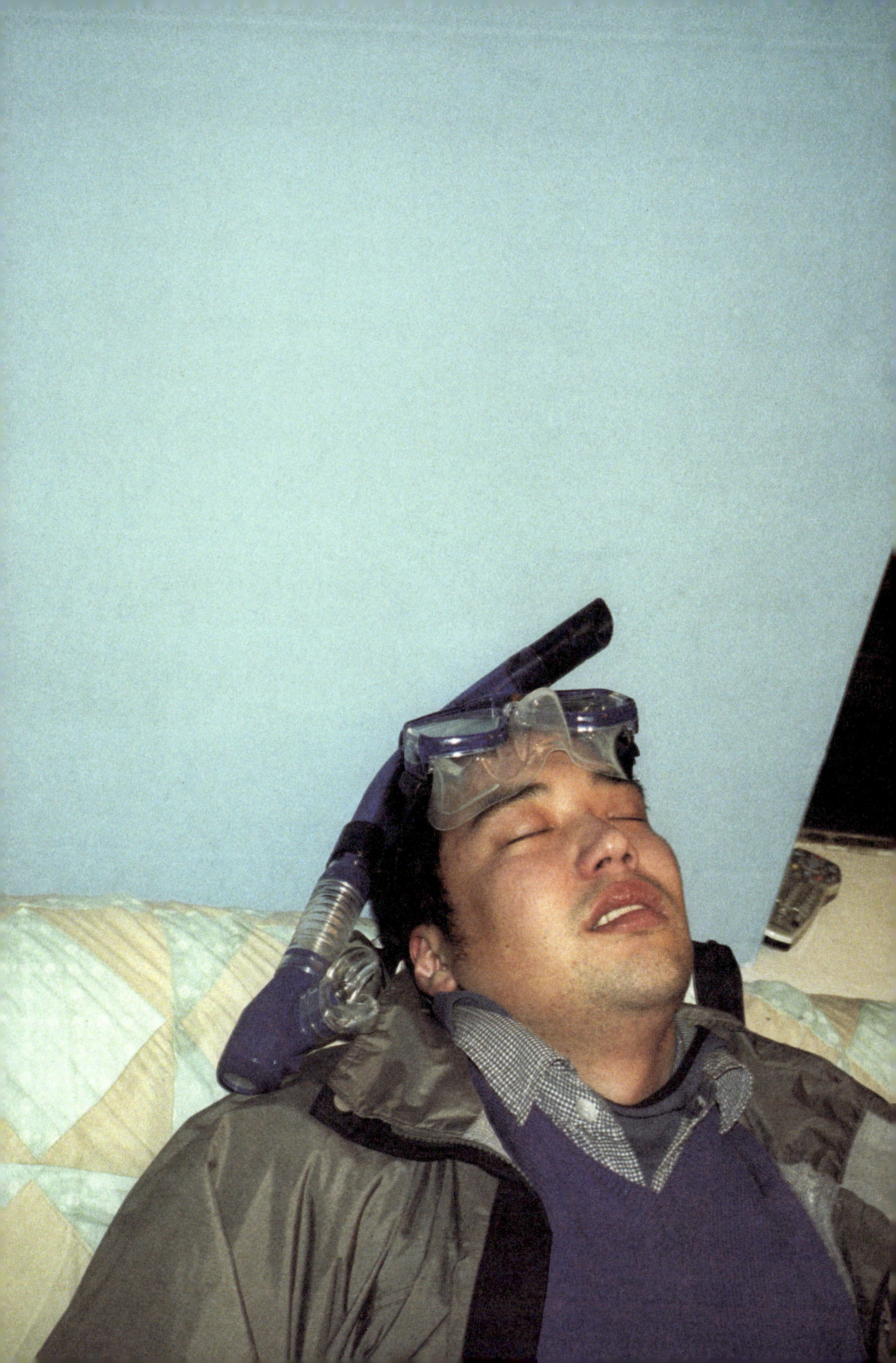

SOHO LAB
ONE WAY
www.can

re.com
Budweiser
KING OF BEERS
CRISP • CLEAN • REFRESHING
N.Y. 1137
SUPREME

METROPLITAN FUNERAL SERVICE

THIS MAN SAYS:
I'll give you
$1.5 billion!
Mafia running out of mobsters
Find out how YOU can join — INSIDE!

Two tons of trouble
for 4 in coke bust

HUGE WAR
PROTEST
GRIPS CITY
SEE PAGES 2-3

SPORTS FINAL
DAILY NEWS
New York's Hometown Newspaper

EXCLUSIVE
American
Gulf War
POWs suing
Iraq for
$900 million

TORTURED
BY SADDAM
SEE PAGES 6-7

IT'S TIME TO
"SNEAKY

ENGINE
ENAMEL

smoke, eat or drink

BLOW
Dash

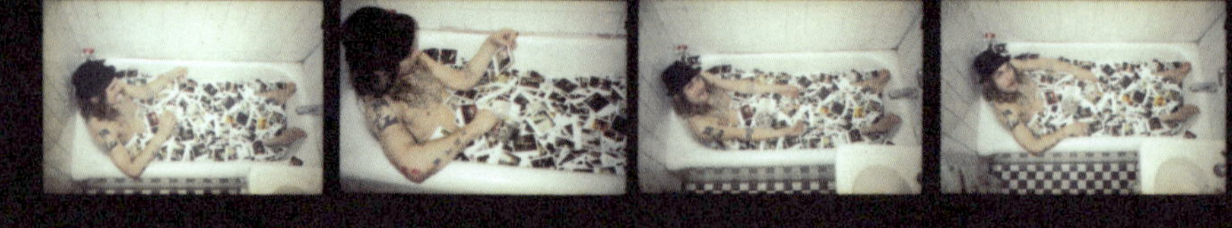
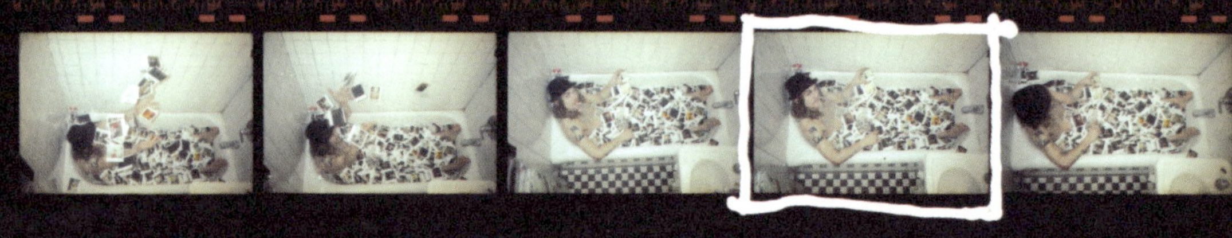

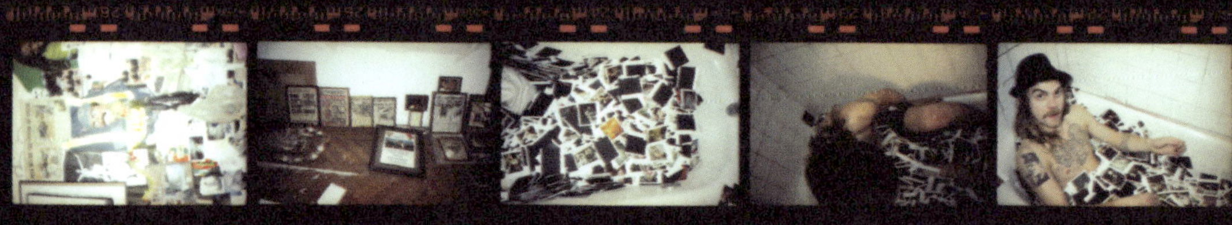

CENTER
DEVELOPING
FREE
PHOTO CENTER
FILM DEVELOPING
2" SET FREE
4" JUMBO PRINTS
NO EXTRA CHARGE
12 EXP. $1.99
24 EXP. 5.99
36 EXP. 6.99
FREE
5x7 8x10
AriZona

Florence Rush

its lookin' up folks. i love you.

Thanks to...
Nick Neubeck, Dash Snow, Jesse, Kenji, Kent, Nikko, Scott from Saved Tattoo, Cheryl Dunn, Leroy Neiman,
The Squirrels of Thompkins Square Park,
all that appear in this book, and the Contax T2 camera that gave it's life for this project.